Grannie Jus' Come!

*In most loving memory of Sophia Aurora Graham
Harewood, my Grannie Sophie.* —A.S.

Dedicated to my daughter Mayakisha. —K.L.

Grannie Jus' Come!

Story by **Ana Sisnett** ✦ Pictures by **Karen Lusebrink**

Children's Book Press   San Francisco, California

Is Tuesday afternoon.
Grannie always come!

Is Tuesday after lunch.
Grannie soon come!

Look! Over dere, yu see?
Grannie bus jus' come!

She 'ave on the new shoes Mommie give to her.
"Dey fit me foot comfortable and nice yu see!"

She 'ave on the new dress Auntie sen' for her.

She 'ave on her glasses; dey 'ave gol' rim.
"Protect me eyes from too much wind!"

She 'ave on her everyday, wide-brim blue straw hat.
"For sun beat hot, hot, hot; no good for head top."

She 'ave on her everyday two-strap blue purse.
In it: bus fare, kerchief, glasscase,
peppermint candy, an' melcoche for three.
Grannie say, "Yu mus' share!"

Melcoche is a very sweet, golden-brown stick candy.

Is Tuesday afternoon
an' Grannie jus' come!

"Come Grannie come, si' down right 'ere;
come tek a lickle res'.
Put down yu purse an' tek off yu hat."

"Tek off yu glasses; put dem in de case.
Tek off yu shoes an' yu pretty new dress.
Put Daddy slippers on an' Mommie housedress."

"Yu wan' some water? Yu wan' some tea?"
She say, "T'ank yu, t'ank yu me luv; yu sweet like sugar!
But please for some juice an' vanilla wafer, two!"
Is Tuesday after lunch an' my Grannie jus' come!

"Oh, Grannie," Ah say, "yu smell so good!"
She say, "A lickle talcum powder sprinkle 'ere an' 'ere is all,
but t'ank yu, t'ank yu me luv."

"Oh, Grannie," Ah say, "yu skin so soft!"
She say, "Lickle cold cream an' rose water is all,
but t'ank yu, t'ank yu me luv!"

"Oh, Grannie," Ah say, "yu hair so white!"
She say, "A good washin' an' blue rinse is all, yu like it?
T'ank yu, t'ank yu me luv!"

Ah say, "Oh, Grannie! Ah luv yu so much!"
She say, "From de very first time Ah set eyes 'pon yu,
Ah did luv yu plenty, plenty me luv!"

Is Tuesday afternoon
an my Grannie jus' come!

I WAS BORN in the town of Paraíso in the Central American country of Panama. My grandparents came to Panama from Jamaica and Barbados, islands in the Caribbean. I grew up speaking Caribbean English, and I also spoke Spanish.

When I was almost thirteen, I moved to the United States to live with relatives. I still talked the way I did in Panama and some of the children at school used to say to me, "You talk funny." I felt sad, angry, even embarrassed because I didn't want people to say things like that about how I talked. And you know what? I thought my new friends sounded pretty funny, too! Soon, however, I began to learn new words and ways of saying things and I mixed them together with my Caribbean English accent.

Although I haven't lived in Panama for a long time, many people say they can still hear my accent, and I like that. It makes me feel proud of my family and friends, of our history—of who I am and where I come from. I like to speak and write in Caribbean English, and I use it to share special thoughts and memories that I carry inside me. I wrote this book so that you, too, could have a chance to visit with my dear Grannie Sophie—my mother's mother whom I loved so much.

Come, les' sit on de step in front our house. Grannie bus soon come!   —*Ana Sisnett*

Ana Sisnett is a spoken-word artist, writer, and activist. Inspired by the oral traditions of the African diaspora, she explores poetry-rhythm-sound-stories in English, Spanish, and the Caribbean English dialect that she spoke at home in her native community of Paraíso, Panama. She now lives in Austin, Texas.

Karen Lusebrink works as a muralist, and is also an artist, designer, and dancer. She has created posters and costumes for the San Francisco Carnaval, and teaches art and reading to children. Karen and her daughter Mayakisha live in San Francisco, California.

Story copyright © 1997 by Ana Sisnett. All rights reserved.   Pictures copyright © 1997 by Karen Lusebrink. All rights reserved.
Editors: Harriet Rohmer and David Schecter   Design and Production: Cathleen O'Brien   Editorial/Production Assistant: Laura Atkins

T'ank yu, t'ank yu! Paraíso and Panama friends and family; Arlene, Catfish Poets, David, Harriet and Children's Book Press; Dottie, Gisèle, Karen B., Jasmin, Eva and RV, Dawn, the Fifis, Josh, my Auntie Nita, Randi, Suzanne, my brothers Tito and Chip, and my uncles Peach, Henry, Slim, Vic, and their families; Daddy—Yu sweet no sugar! Victor, Jr., Morgan, Alana, and Deshawn; my "babies," Meredith and Ghamal; Mom, from the apple of your eye; and Sandy, for your visions of this book and love for me. —A.S.

Thank you to Harriet Rohmer, Laura Atkins, and Cathleen O'Brien, Carolina Lozano, Ingrid Lusebrink, Dr. Vija B. Lusebrink, Anita Lusebrink, Irene and Alexandria Cordova, Evans and Brown. —K.L.

Thanks to the staff of Children's Book Press: Janet Levin, Emily Romero, Stephanie Sloan, and Christina Tarango.

Children's Book Press is a nonprofit publisher of multicultural literature for children, supported in part by grants from the California Arts Council. Write us for a complimentary catalog: Children's Book Press, 246 First Street, Suite 101, San Francisco, CA 94105.

Distributed to the book trade by Publishers Group West

Library of Congress Cataloging-in-Publication Data
Sisnett, Ana. Grannie jus' come! / story by Ana Sisnett; pictures by Karen Lusebrink.   p.   cm.
Summary: Using Caribbean English a young girl lovingly describes a visit from her grandmother who arrives by bus and looks great in her new shoes and colorful clothes.
ISBN 0-89239-150-2 (hc)   [1. Grandmothers—Fiction. 2. Caribbean Area—Fiction.]
I. Lusebrink, Karen, ill. II. Title.   PZ7.S621955Gr   1997   [E]—dc21   97-436   CIP   AC

Printed in Hong Kong through Marwin Productions
10   9   8   7   6   5   4   3   2   1